JAN – – 2014

# JENNY CRAIG'S
# I Believe in Genevieve

By Jenny Craig

Illustrated by Wendy Edelson

Cataloging-in-Publication data on file with the Library of Congress
ISBN 978-1-62157-085-1

Published in the United States by
Regnery Kids
An imprint of Regnery Publishing, Inc.
One Massachusetts Avenue NW
Washington, DC 20001
www.Regnery.com

Manufactured in the United States of America
10 9 8 7 6 5 4 3 2 1

Books are available in quantity for promotional or premium use. Write to Director of Special Sales, Regnery Publishing, Inc.,
One Massachusetts Avenue NW, Washington, DC 20001, for information on discounts and terms, or call (202) 216-0600.

Distributed to the trade by
Perseus Distribution, 250 West 57th Street, New York, NY 10107

## ∽ Dedication ∽

To my children and grandchildren who continue to remind me of the joys and memories that only a family can produce. I thank them for their love, their support, and their encouragement throughout the years.

To all the children throughout the world who have known the joy of reading, for they have known the excitement of being transported into a world of imagination within the pages of the written word. May these pages inspire you to always be the best that you can be.

To Candy Ride for giving us so many thrills as he gracefully glided around the racetrack…his feet never seeming to touch the ground. I will always cherish the times we stood together in the Winners' Circle.

# Hi there!

My name is Jenny Craig (and, yes, my "real" name is Genevieve). When I was a little girl, I was a lot like the Genevieve in this story.

For one thing, I loved horses. In fact, I still do. I own a stable in Rancho Santa Fe where we train horses for racing. You probably won't be too surprised to learn that one of my favorite horses is named Candy Ride. Candy Ride is now in Kentucky, a father to many foals. He sired a colt named Sidney's Candy. It was a lot of fun to see Sidney's Candy run in the famous Kentucky Derby and Belmont Stakes races. I am sure Candy Ride was just as proud of him as I was! You see, he was named after my husband Sidney.

I also had a big sister named Trudy. I miss her a lot. She was my best friend throughout my entire life. We played together, worked together, and made many wonderful memories together.

Like Genevieve in the story, I learned (a long time ago) that eating healthy foods and staying active can be fun. I have gone on walking trips all over the world. I was able to see fun places while keeping my body active. You can, too! Always remember that any journey starts out with the first step! In fact, my late husband Sid Craig and I helped millions of people learn that lesson too. We opened more than six hundred weight-loss centers all over the world to help people lose weight, make better eating and exercise choices, and, in the process, improve their lives.

If there's one thing I'd like you to remember about this story, it's this: be like Genevieve! Decide what it is that you love to do and go after it. Don't be afraid to dream big. It takes lots of work, and sometimes you may want to quit. But never give up! Make the commitment to work hard in order to achieve whatever it is you hope to accomplish. You are unique—there is no one else exactly like you—so, be the BEST that you can be, and you will lead the way for others. Good luck, and may God bless you with a wonderful life.

Sincerely,

Jenny Craig

Candy Ride

Jenny Craig

"Trudy! Trudy!" Jenny called as she ran up the porch steps. "Look what I'm going to do this summer!"

The flyer in Jenny's hand read: "Summer Riding Camp at Rancho Paseana."

"Looks like fun, Jenny," Trudy said. "There's just one problem, little Miss Genevieve. You don't have a horse."

"Like that's going to stop me!" Jenny said with a flourish.

Bright and early the next morning, Jenny ran down to Rancho Paseana.

"Hey John!" she called out to the stable's owner. "Do you need any help?"

"I only wish I could find some good help, little gal," said John.

"Well, I only wish I could go to your summer riding camp," Jenny exclaimed.

"Well now," John answered. "Sounds like we need to make a little deal here. You help me take care of the horses and clean the stables, and I'll give you a spot at riding camp."

"Sounds great!" said Jenny. "Except, you know I don't have my own horse, right?"

"This must be your lucky day," said John. "It just so happens that the old champ out there in the paddock needs a little extra care. Think you can get him back in shape?"

Jenny nodded vigorously and looked wistfully at the scruffy old horse. It was love at first sight.

"Why, you're as sweet as candy," Jenny declared. "That's it! I'll call you Candy Ride!"

The next morning, Jenny arrived at the stables two hours early. John showed her how to sweep the stables, brush the horses, and fill the water buckets.

As Jenny walked along the stalls, she stopped to get acquainted with each horse. She had come prepared with a pocketful of sugary treats.

"One for you, one for me," Jenny said, offering each horse a sugar treat, then letting another one melt on her own tongue. "Sweet!"

By the time she'd finished making the rounds, Jenny felt sluggish and drowsy. She leaned back on a bale of hay in Candy Ride's stall. Before she knew it, she was fast asleep.

If Candy Ride hadn't nuzzled her shoulder, she would have slept through the first session of riding camp.

Each rider saddled up their horses and led them into the ring. John made them practice some basic training movements.

Candy Ride did okay walking. He had a little trouble trotting. But, whoa, was he good at standing still!

After the session ended and the horses were tended, the hot and thirsty riders were treated to some of their favorite snacks—soda, cookies, and candy. All the kids gobbled up the goodies—except for a golden-haired girl who was sipping from a bottle of water.

The next day, Jenny spotted the blond-haired girl trotting into the ring. She was the best rider that Jenny had ever seen. Her posture was perfect and her horse was shiny and beautifully groomed.

"That's Olivia and her horse, Buck," whispered one of the riders. "They always win every ribbon."

Jenny was mesmerized by their moves. Olivia and Buck trotted and cantered so effortlessly.

Jenny patted Candy Ride.

"We may be slow and out of shape now, but just you wait and see," she said with determination.

Later that week Jenny talked Trudy into going to camp with her.

"We've got to figure out why Olivia and Buck are so good," Jenny said.

The girls tried not to be too obvious as they peeked into Buck's stall. Olivia talked gently to him as she combed out his mane and tail and cleaned his hooves.

At first, Jenny and Trudy didn't see anything out of the ordinary. But then, Olivia offered her horse a bucket of food. Buck gobbled it up in record time!

"What's in that bucket?" Jenny blurted out, startling Olivia.

"Oh, it's a special blend of oats, corn, barley, and bran," Olivia smiled. "For an extra treat, sometimes I add an apple or a couple of carrots."

Jenny asked, "How many sugar cubes do you give Buck?"

"I don't give him sweets like that," Olivia answered. "He gets all the energy he needs from these healthy vegetables and grains. It's actually pretty yummy. Want a taste?"

"Seriously?" Trudy asked, cautiously taking a teeny tiny bite.

But Jenny was all in. She grabbed a handful and said, "Why not? If it works for you and Buck, we're game."

Jenny, Trudy, and their new best friend Olivia stayed after practice that day to watch the older riders go through their programs.

"Wow!" said Jenny. "Do you think I'll ever ride that well?"

"You're already better than I was when I first started," Olivia admitted. "I was such a weakling that my instructor made me lift bales of hay until my arms felt like they would fall off. He even made me do the same running and jumping workout that the horses did!"

"No wonder you're the best rider in our camp!" said Jenny.

"It took a lot of work to get strong enough to handle Buck. He was a wild thing when we first started out together," Olivia said.

"We had better get going," Trudy said. "Mom's expecting us home for dinner soon."

Olivia called after them, "Don't forget your veggies!"

They all laughed and waved good-bye.

"I sure would like to ride as well as Olivia does some day!" said Jenny.

"You can do it, Jenny," said Trudy. "It sounds like it has taken Olivia a lot of practice and hard work to become a great rider."

"But where do I start?" asked Jenny.

"Look at this," Trudy said, showing Jenny a picture of delicious vegetables.

"I'm not crazy about vegetables," Jenny confessed. "But those look good enough to eat!"

"I've been thinking," Trudy said. "Olivia's horse perked right up after eating that healthy stuff she gave him. I wonder if eating more vegetables and grains would do the same for us?"

"Makes sense to me," said Jenny. "Since you love to cook so much, why don't you come up with a plan?"

The next morning, Jenny woke up to the sound of the blender whirring away in the kitchen.

"Oh good!" said Trudy. "You're just in time to try my new creation. I call it the Trudy Fruity."

She handed Jenny a big glass of something creamy, frothy, and very purple.

"Drink it!" Trudy demanded in her bossiest big sister voice.

"Okay, okay!" Jenny took her first sip. "*Mmmm!* This is the most delicious milkshake I've ever had!"

"Ha! Tricked you! It's a smoothie, not a milkshake," Trudy said. "It has all kinds of healthy stuff in it like yogurt and fruit. Blueberries and strawberries are what make it oh-so-good for you."

"It's the breakfast of horse champions!" Trudy said with a giggle. "Here, try some of this, too." Trudy handed Jenny a piece of whole-wheat toast slathered with peanut butter.

Jenny gave her sister a quick hug and said, "Trudy, I hereby proclaim you my summer camp chef!"

When Olivia arrived at the stable that day, Jenny was already there. She and John were stacking bales of hay and arranging jumps in a circle around the riding ring.

"What's all this?" asked Olivia.

"Surprise!" called Jenny. "It's our very own 'ob-stable' course! Get it? After we talked, I thought it might be fun to try jumping the course ourselves."

"Have at it, girls!" said John. "Our big show is just a month away."

Jenny cranked up the music on her cell phone and they were off—running, jumping, and lifting bales of hay.

To help Jenny with her chores, they added a water-bucket shuffle and a stable "sweep-da-bop" to their routine.

As other riders trickled in and saw how much fun Olivia and Jenny were having, they all joined in.

The whole team was rosy-cheeked and giggling when John came in and said, "Now, let's give those horses a workout!"

The days flew by! Finally, there was just one more day until the horse show. Jenny was brushing out Candy Ride after an especially good practice session. The horse's big brown eyes sparkled, and he was strong, full of energy, and absolutely beautiful.

Olivia peered over the stable wall and said, "Wow, Jenny. It's amazing. He doesn't even look like the same worn-out horse you started with."

Jenny put her arms around Candy Ride and cooed into his ear, "Yeah, but I knew you were a champ the first time I laid eyes on you."

The next morning, Jenny woke up with a bad case of horse-show jitters. "What was I thinking?" she moaned to Trudy. "I can't go out there and ride in front of all those people."

"Come on, little sis," encouraged Trudy. "You can do this! Just look at how far you've come. I believe in you, Genevieve."

"You do?" Jenny looked into the mirror. The girl looking back at her was strong and healthy. Her hair was shiny, her cheeks rosy, and her eyes twinkly.

"I do! And you should, too," Trudy said. "Now, repeat after me: I believe in Genevieve, I believe in Genevieve…"

The two girls were still chanting those words as Trudy led Jenny out of the house and down the road to Rancho Paseana.

Jenny became more and more excited as she watched each one of her teammates ride the course. Everyone was doing a terrific job.

"Next up is Genevieve riding Candy Ride!" the announcer said.

Jenny whispered, "I believe in Genevieve. I believe in Genevieve." Then, giving her horse a pat, she said, "And I believe in you, too, Candy Ride."

Jenny and Candy Ride went through each part of the program without a hitch. If the big smiles on John and Trudy's faces were any sign, they must have done a good job.

" 'Atta girl!" John shouted.

"Told you so," said Trudy.

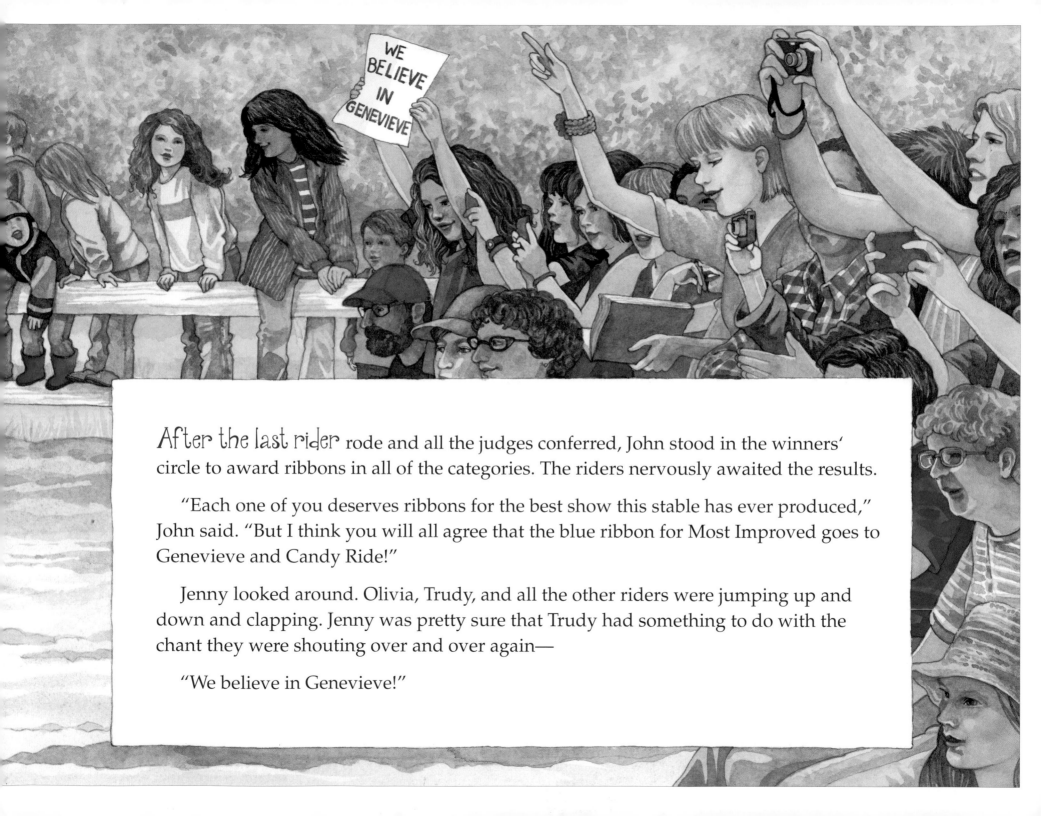

After the last rider rode and all the judges conferred, John stood in the winners' circle to award ribbons in all of the categories. The riders nervously awaited the results.

"Each one of you deserves ribbons for the best show this stable has ever produced," John said. "But I think you will all agree that the blue ribbon for Most Improved goes to Genevieve and Candy Ride!"

Jenny looked around. Olivia, Trudy, and all the other riders were jumping up and down and clapping. Jenny was pretty sure that Trudy had something to do with the chant they were shouting over and over again—

"We believe in Genevieve!"

# Jenny's "Ob-Stable" Course

In the story, getting fit and eating healthy brought out the very best in both Genevieve and Candy Ride. You don't have to have a horse to achieve the same results at home!

Find a big open space and set up your own obstacle course. Use pillows, brightly colored paper, or whatever you can to mark your course (unless, of course, you happen to have a few bales of hay handy). Crank up your favorite music and off you go!

➤ Wiggle and Stretch—warm up your muscles

➤ Walk around the circuit 2 times

➤ Stop and Jump—do 10 jumping jacks

➤ Skip around the circuit 2 times

➤ Stop and Drop—do 10 push-ups

➤ Jog around the circuit 2 times

➤ Stop and Sit—do 10 sit-ups

➤ Now go, go, go!

➤ Run around the circuit 4 times

➤ Start at the beginning and do it again!

After completion, cool down your muscles with gentle twists and turns, walking in place until you catch your breath.

# Trudy's Good Goodies

## ~ Trudy Fruity Smoothie ~

1 cup yogurt
1 cup frozen berries (strawberries, raspberries, blueberries)
1 banana
Ice or juice diluted with water

Optional:
Almond or peanut butter
Protein powder

Combine yogurt, berries, and banana in a blender. Blend until smooth. Pour into a glass and enjoy. It's delicious!

## Horsing Around ~ Snacks ~

If you happen to be lucky enough to have a horse in your life, there are several snacks both of you can share.

Apples
Bananas
Carrot sticks

Rolled oat bites "glued" together with a little molasses or honey.

## ～ Hit the Yummy Trail Mix ～

Pick and choose your favorite healthy ingredients to make your own "hit the yummy trail mix."

### 1 PART CRUNCH

Whole-grain cereal
Pretzels
Popcorn (minus the butter
   and salt)
Sesame sticks
Granola

### 1 PART SCRUNCH

Raisins (plain or yogurt-
   covered)
Dried cranberries or cherries
Banana chips
Coconut shavings
Chocolate chips (white, milk, or
   dark chocolate)
Carob chips
M&Ms

### 1 PART MUNCH

Sunflower seeds
Almond slivers
Pumpkin seeds

Grab small handfuls of whatever you have available, mix them together, and crunch, scrunch, munch!

# Trudy's Good Goodies

## Candy Ride Pops

Seedless grapes (red, purple, or green)

4" carrot sticks, cut into thin strips

Stick one carrot stick into one grape; place pops in an ice tray and freeze as long as you want—a few hours for a mushy treat, a whole day or two for a popsicle-style snack.

## ~ Fruity Fence Posts ~

Pick three to five of your favorite fresh fruits:

Bananas, apples, cherries, strawberries, oranges, pineapple, kiwi, blueberries, raspberries

Wash fruit and, very carefully (with adult supervision), slice the fruit into bite-sized pieces. Slide fruit onto wooden or bamboo skewers or long toothpicks. Mix and match the fruit to make colorful patterns.

# Giddy Up and Make Healthy Choices

## Ten Fun Ways to Get Up and Go!

1. Play tag at recess

2. Take a walk around your neighborhood or a nearby park with friends or family

3. Dance to your favorite music

4. Challenge a friend to a race (run, skip, hop, or walk backward)

5. Join a sports team at school or your local community center (soccer, tennis, swimming—there's sure to be something you'll enjoy)

6. Play catch or kickball with a friend

7. See how many times you can jump a rope without missing

8. Clean your room from top to bottom as fast as you can (Ready? Set? Go!)

9. Take the stairs and see if you can reach your destination faster than if you took the elevator or escalator

10. March in place or do jumping jacks every time a commercial comes on during a TV show

Do like the song in the "Madagascar" movie says and "move it, move it!"

## Ten Great Snacks to Grab and Go!

1. Fruit (take your pick!)

2. Granola bar

3. String cheese

4. Whole-grain crackers

5. Celery sticks spread with peanut butter and dotted with raisins

6. Carrot sticks

7. Popcorn (replace butter with a sprinkle of parmesan cheese)

8. Yogurt

9. Rice cake topped with peanut butter, cream cheese, or honey

10. Whole-wheat toast or English muffin

Make sure to wash it down with lots of $H_2O$!

# I Believe in Me!

Draw or insert a picture of you looking your very best.

# Acknowledgments

Many thanks to my dear friend Cheryl Barnes for believing that children would be inspired by my story. I am indeed honored that you felt my story worthy enough to be told.

To Wendy Edelson for her wonderful talent of illustration that colorfully brings my story to life. I envy her gift while I still struggle with stick figures. Thank you for the many hours you spent making each illustration so perfect to tell the story where words alone were not enough.

My thanks to the wonderful team at Regnery who poured so much creative energy into this project. Special thanks to the publisher, Marji Ross, and my editor, Diane Lindsey Reeves, for your suggestions, commitment, and confidence in the project. My deepest appreciation to Amanda Larsen for your artful page design and to publicist Ryan Pando.

Thanks to Gail Kileen, my assistant, for her help in searching for pictures and working with the editor to hasten the process. Gail, when I look in the dictionary under "right hand," I see your picture.

My thanks to the millions of clients throughout the world who have enriched my life with their stories of successful lifestyle changes. You made hard work meaningful as I looked forward to each day. Without your contribution to my success, I would not be writing this book.